Walt Disney Productions...

The STRONGEST MAN in the WORLD

Adapted by MEL CEBULASH
from the Walt Disney motion picture

SCHOLASTIC BOOK SERVICES
New York Toronto London Auckland Sydney Tokyo

For my old man—in memory of the weights.

Other books by the author available
from Scholastic Book Services:
  *THE BOATNIKS
  *THE LOVE BUG
  *HERBIE RIDES AGAIN
   dic-tion-ar-y skilz
   MAN IN THE GREEN BERET AND OTHER MEDAL
   OF HONOR WINNERS

  *Adapted from Walt Disney motion pictures

14 13 12 11 10 9 8 7 6 5 4 3   5 6 7 8 9/7 0/8
                Printed in the U.S.A.

The Strongest Man In the World

CHAPTER ONE

Dean Higgins limped into his Medfield College office. As usual, his foot hurt. It hurt so much that he limped past Medfield's Regent and slumped into a chair in the corner of his office.

Regent Dietz watched Higgins remove his shoe and sock and begin wrapping his toe with a bandage. As Higgins continued, the Regent's watchful gaze turned into a cold stare.

"Oh, does that hurt!" Dean Higgins said. "It's unbelievable how much pain a little thing like this can give you."

Higgins looked up. "Have you ever had a corn?" he asked.

"No," Regent Dietz answered angrily. "I never had a corn!"

The Regent's show of anger puzzled Higgins. "Sir," he said, "I know it's a bit hot today and people are somewhat out of sorts, but you shouldn't be mad at me just because I have a bad corn on my foot."

"I'm not mad at you because you have a corn on your foot," the Regent corrected. "I'm mad because I have something important to say and I haven't been able to get it out because of your foot. I'm either hearing about it or watching you limp around on it. Now, will you sit down!"

Higgins quickly moved behind his desk and sat down.

"I have a message from the Board of Regents," Dietz said.

"Oh, good! How is the Board of Regents these days?"

"Disappointed," said Dietz. "They feel the problems here at the school are overwhelming."

"So do I," said Higgins. "Why, if I didn't spend the energy I do in watching every penny, we would be down the financial drain right now."

"That's the point. You *are* down the financial drain."

"*I* am," Higgins said, hoping he had heard wrong. "Don't you mean *we* are?"

The Regent shook his head. "No," he said, "I mean *you* are. And the Board wants action! The Board wants new blood, fresh ideas, top level changes. And frankly, I agree."

It sounded like a good move to Higgins. "Good thinking, Dietz!" he exclaimed. "New blood, fresh ideas, top level changes—that's the ticket."

"Glad to hear you agree," said Dietz, almost smiling. "When are you leaving?"

The question lifted Higgins right out of his seat. He limped around the room, wondering if he had heard right. Finally, he asked, "You didn't really mean *top* level changes, did you?"

"Yes, top level, Higgins."

"Not the very tippy, tippy, tippy top?" Higgins asked hopefully.

"Yes, I'm afraid so," Dietz explained. "Let's face it, Higgins, you've had years to get this place on its feet and you haven't done it. You waste, waste, waste! Why, the costs for your Science Department alone are ridiculous."

"That's that Quigley again," Higgins said anxiously. "I'll fire him! That will be the end of the waste; I'll guarantee it. Out with Quigley, out with waste. You'll see."

"Dean Higgins, let's not make a problem out of this. Why don't you step down gracefully?"

"Step down?" Higgins repeated. "I can't do that now in the middle of my promotional program. I'm going to raise money. Money's what you want, isn't it?"

"Yes, but how?" Dietz asked.

"Don't ask," Higgins warned. "That's my business. That's why I'm here, and all I need is thirty days. Just thirty short days. Okay?"

"All right," Dietz said slowly. "But that's it. No excuses this time. And even at that, I don't know what I'm going to tell the Board of Regents."

"Sir," Higgins said, leading the Regent to the door, "you'll find your confidence in me will be amply rewarded."

"I have no confidence in you," Dietz corrected. "But you have your thirty days, so do something. Above all, get some order restored around this place; and no more expensive nonsense."

"I assure you there is no nonsense going on," Higgins said, as the two men stepped through his outer office. "If there were, I would notice it. Nothing escapes my eyes."

Higgins stopped. He looked through the glass door at something down the corridor and froze in horror. If Dietz also saw it, his thirty days would be thirty seconds. He turned quickly and pushed the Regent back into the office.

"What are you doing?" Dietz asked.

"You forgot something," Higgins said, glancing around the room and spotting his own hat on the coat rack. "You forgot your hat. Here, let me get it for you."

"Thank you," Dietz said, without thinking.

Then Dietz set the hat on his head and turned to look at it in the mirror. At the same time, Higgins sneaked a peek down the corridor. The "thing" was disappearing around a corner.

"Wait a minute!" Dietz roared. "This isn't my hat. As a matter of fact, I wasn't wearing a hat."

"That's right," Higgins said. "What are you doing with my hat?"

Dietz handed him the hat and said, "What's the matter with you, Higgins?"

"I'm fine," Higgins said.

Then Higgins heard it. It was distant. It was faint. But it was a M-O-O-O! Higgins held his stomach and doubled over slightly, as the Regent turned to him.

"Did you hear that?" Higgins said, as if he were in pain. "Maybe there is something the matter with me, after all. Well, good-bye, Regent Dietz, and tell the Board of Regents to cheer up. Every cloud has a silver lining."

For a second, the Regent stared coldly at Higgins, who was recollecting the "thing" he had seen in the corridor. He shuddered to think what might have happened had Dietz spotted a cow going through the hall. Terror suddenly seized him! The cow was still inside the school!

The Strongest Man In the World

CHAPTER TWO

The cow had already been inside the school for some time. She was safely, if not happily, housed in the science lab. Ruthybelle was her name, and she was the skinniest cow within miles of Medfield.

Ruthybelle was the center of science lab activity. It was Richard Schuyler's "Creative Lab Month," and with the help of the other students, he hoped to create a "super" food to fatten up Ruthybelle.

Dexter, one of Schuyler's classmates, had come up with a liquid formula, and while Dean Higgins was following the cow's trail through the school, Dexter was trying to get Ruthybelle to taste his creation.

Ruthybelle didn't like the concoction in the bowl that Dexter was holding in front of her. She kept turning away. Finally, Dexter sniffed the bowl. He wrinkled his nose at the smell.

"I'm not sure a cow twice as starved as Ruthybelle would have anything to do with this stuff," Dexter announced.

Schuyler rushed over and stuck his finger in the bowl. Then he licked his finger. "It's probably that acid taste she doesn't like," he said.

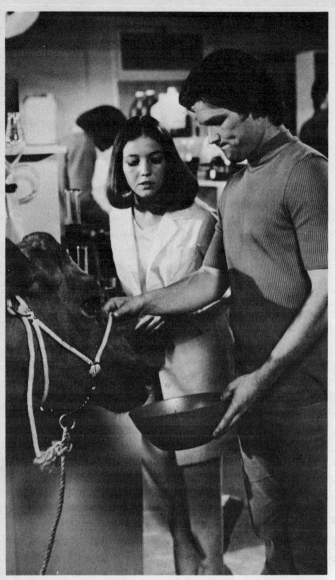

Ruthybelle may be only a cow, but boy is she a fussy eater! She doesn't like the concoction that Dexter is holding in front of her and refuses to eat it.

"Get rid of that and she'll probably take it."

Then Dexter stuck his finger into the bowl and licked the solution off it. "Yeah," he said in agreement. "Maybe you're right."

Schuyler slapped Dexter on the back and said, "Well, back to my vitamins."

Schuyler strutted away, and Debbie, another student, stared after him. Then she said to Dexter, "Boy, is he acting like the big man around here."

"Well, it *was* his idea," Dexter explained. "And Professor Quigley thought we should try it out. After all, if we could find a way to beef up cattle in our state, we'd really be doing something."

Debbie was listening to Dexter, but she was watching Schuyler who was across the room cheerfully dumping vitamins into a meat grinder. "It would be a good idea," she answered, "but do you think he really knows what he's doing with all those vitamins?"

Schuyler certainly didn't appear to know what he was doing, but that fact didn't bother Dexter. "Sure he knows what he's doing," he told Debbie. "He's been studying up a lot on vitamins lately. Quigley has a lot of confidence in him."

Just then a person with no confidence in any person or thing in the science lab came crashing into the room. It was Dean Higgins. "Where is he?" he asked Dexter.

Noticing the Dean's limp, Dexter said, "What happened to your foot?"

"Never mind my foot!" Dean Higgins roared. "Just tell me where he is."

"Who?"

"Quigley. Who do you think, *who*?"

"Oh, he'll be a few minutes late," Dexter explained. "He dropped by the supply room to pick up some more test tubes."

The Dean couldn't believe his ears. "You mean he leaves you people alone?" he asked.

"He sure does," Schuyler said proudly. "We're on the honor system."

Before Higgins could answer, Ruthybelle added a loud MOO-OO-OO to Schuyler's words.

"I suppose *that's* on the honor system, too," Higgins said, motioning in Ruthybelle's direction.

"A cow on the honor system," Schuyler said, laughing and hoping to get some of the anger out of the Dean's voice. "That's a pretty good one, Dean Higgins."

"Don't try to butter me up," Higgins warned. "This isn't funny."

Breaking in, Dexter said, "Dean Higgins, can we do anything for you?"

"No you can't," Higgins said. "I just came up here to make a little announcement. So you can all get back to work."

"Maybe he's going to give Quigley a promotion," Debbie whispered to Dexter.

"Yeah," Dexter said. "That would be something."

Higgins wandered around the lab, trying hard to imagine what was going on. Finally, he stopped by Schuyler who was still running vitamins through the meat grinder.

"Do you think it would be too much," Higgins began, "if I asked you what you're doing?"

Schuyler stopped his grinding. "Of course not," he answered. Then he went back to work.

"Well, what *are* you doing?" shouted Higgins.

"I'm crushing up vitamins," Schuyler said.

"I can see that much!" Higgins roared. "But what for?"

"Oh, for the cow, sir," Schuyler explained. "Everything we do around here is for the cow."

Higgins was afraid he *had* heard correctly this time. "You mean to tell me that you are taking perfectly good vitamins and crushing them up and feeding them to that cow?"

"Yes, sir," Schuyler said, swelling with enthusiasm. "That's how we're going to cure Ruthybelle of her nutritional problem. As you can see, she's rather skinny. But, if we're successful, we'll end up with a fat cow."

"So that's what all this expense is about," Higgins muttered to himself, "making a cow fat."

"Not only fat, sir," Schuyler corrected, "but strong too. Isn't it thrilling?"

The Dean watched as Schuyler stuck his finger into the formula and then tasted it.

"Thrilled?" Higgins repeated. "I'm overwhelmed."

"I thought you would be," Schuyler said, totally unaware of the Dean's attempt at sarcasm. "It was really my idea, but all the kids are helping out."

Schuyler turned to Gilbert who was warming a pizza over a Bunsen burner nearby. "Hey, Gilbert," he called. "Would you bring me another piece of pizza? This doesn't have quite enough flavor yet."

"Sure," Gilbert said, springing into action. "One piece of pizza coming up."

Coming up to the meat grinder, Gilbert dropped the piece of pizza into the machine and Schuyler ground it up.

Higgins' eyes almost bulged out of his head. "Pizza?" he said in amazement. "A cow eating pizza?"

"She seems to like it, too," Schuyler said. "Do you think she might be Italian?"

Schuyler always loved his own jokes, and this was no exception. He laughed and laughed. Finally, Higgins screamed, "That's not funny, Schuyler! Not at all funny!"

Still laughing, Schuyler said, "Don't you get it — an Italian cow eating pizza. An Italian cow — that's the part that kills me."

Schuyler laughed again. His little joke was certainly funny to him, and to Professor Quigley who entered the lab and came up behind Higgins, it appeared that his student and the Dean were sharing the fun.

"Glad to see you're having a good time, Dean Higgins," Quigley said.

Higgins turned and said, "He is. I'm not."

The smile disappeared from Quigley's face and he said, "Sorry about that, but it's nice of you to come. May I show you around?"

"I don't want to be shown around," Higgins snarled. "I've just been through plenty already with that vitamin-grinding meathead that calls himself a science major!"

Schuyler was close enough to catch the Dean's words, and he said, "I heard that, sir."

"Good," Higgins answered, and turning to Quigley, he added, "And that's not all I have to say!"

Just then, Debbie and Dexter joined the little group, and Debbie said, "Here comes the announcement."

Higgins didn't know what she meant, but he had no time to figure it out. "Quigley," he said, "do you have any idea what this thing — this operation — is costing us?"

"Well, not really," Quigley explained. "But we care and are cutting everywhere we can. Now, take the cow rental for example."

"Cow rental?" Higgins roared. "Do you mean to tell me we are paying money to make a cow fat?"

"You don't want us to have skinny cows, do you, sir?" Debbie asked.

"Who cares?" yelled Higgins.

"Sir," Quigley said helplessly, "try not to get excited."

"Excited?" Higgins repeated. "I'm not excited. Who could be excited? But just tell me how much rental we're paying for that so-called cow."

Quigley swallowed and said, "Not much, sir."

"How much, Quigley?"

"Would fifteen dollars a day be too much?"

"Fifteen dollars a day!" Higgins said painfully. "That's extravagance! That's the kind of thing that's bothering the Board of Regents."

All eyes were on the Dean, waiting for him to continue. No one noticed that the so-called cow had planted her foot on Higgins' sore toe, and the hoof was grinding into it. They did notice Higgins turning red, though.

"He's sure having trouble getting out that announcement," Dexter said to Debbie.

Finally, the cow moved, and Higgins screamed, "Quigley, you're fired!"

"Fired!" Quigley said in disbelief, as Higgins started for the door.

The students crowded after Higgins, and Dexter said, "But what about his promotion?"

Higgins stopped. "Promotion!" he said in disbelief. Then he turned back to Quigley. "As soon as you can, Quigley! Out, out, out!"

The Dean was through the door before anyone could answer. The students couldn't believe their ears. They walked over to their disheartened professor. Then the lab door swung open again. It was Higgins. "And as far as you kids are concerned," he said, "you'd better forget about fat cows and figure out some way to make money for this school because in thirty days, I go. And if I go, you go — all of you! I'll see to that!"

Then Higgins slammed the lab door very hard. It was an exit worth remembering, but the students had other things on their minds at the moment.

"He acts like he's gone crazy," Dexter said.

"I think I can explain it," Quigley answered. "The school has some rather large financial problems. In fact, it may be going under, and the Board of Regents has been putting Dean Higgins under a lot of pressure."

"But what's he going to do without you?" Debbie asked.

"Oh, I'm sure the school can get along without me," Quigley said. "But for now, I suppose we should get Ruthybelle back to the Willoughby farm and tell Silas Willoughby we won't be needing her any more."

While this brief conversation was going on in one part of the lab, a very strange thing was happening elsewhere in the lab.

The strange chain of events was set in motion when Higgins slammed the door. The shock tipped Dexter's chemical solution and it spilled into a transformer. The transformer's electrical pulses gave the solution an eerie green glow. Then a few drops of the formula spilled into Schuyler's vitamin bowl. For a second, the entire bowl glowed. Then the glow faded.

It was a strange event, and it wasn't over. Ruthybelle wandered over to the vitamin bowl and took a few mouthfuls from it.

The skinny old cow's eyes lit up and she spun around. Then a puff of smoke — looking almost as if it were the result of a tiny atomic bomb blast — came out of Ruthybelle's nostrils.

Unfortunately, the whole strange thing happened so quickly that the students and Professor Quigley missed it. It was all over by the time Dexter came over to Ruthybelle and sadly started to lead her out of the lab and back to Silas Willoughby's farm. Dexter was understandably preoccupied, so he certainly couldn't be blamed for missing the strange new look that had come over Ruthybelle's face.

The Strongest Man In the World

CHAPTER THREE

Very late that night, Dexter received a telephone call from Silas Willoughby. The farmer was wide awake and excited about the change that had come over Ruthybelle.

"We didn't do anything," Dexter said, unable to pull himself fully out of the sound sleep the call had interrupted.

"Well, somebody did something to her," Willoughby said. "She's already given eighteen gallons of milk and she's still going strong. What do you think of that?"

Dexter wasn't thinking of anything but sleep. "Good night, Ruthybelle," he said and hung up the phone.

Dexter didn't remember the phone call in the morning, and Schuyler didn't remember that he had dumped his bowl of vitamins back into a cereal box and returned it to his kitchen cabinet. And both of them, of course, knew nothing of the strange series of events set in motion by Dean Higgins' angry slamming of the lab door.

Schuyler was frying some eggs when Dexter asked, "How about letting me borrow some of your cereal?"

"Sure," Schuyler said. "Help yourself."

Dexter helped himself to a bowlful of the

"new" cereal, and just before he tasted it, he said to Schuyler, "It's sure tough about Quigley having to leave the school. The place won't be the same without him."

Then as Dexter began eating, Schuyler said, "I wouldn't worry about that. This isn't the first time that Higgins has fired Quigley. I can remember his being fired at least five times since I've been here."

Dexter didn't hear any part of Schuyler's answer. He was thinking about the puff of blue smoke that had just come out of his nostrils, and he was staring at the snapping, crackling cereal in his bowl. He wasn't sure what was going on, but whatever it was, it frightened him.

Dexter put the unfinished bowl of cereal into the sink and headed for his room. Something very strange was happening to him. He couldn't tell what it was, but he could feel it.

Dexter got a clue when he was tying his shoe laces. One lace snapped in his hand. He puzzled for a moment over the lace, but the time for his first-period class was fast approaching. He quickly got ready and returned to the kitchen in time to see Schuyler setting the cereal bowl on the floor.

"Come on, Brutus, breakfast," Schuyler said to the students' little house pet. Then he said to Dexter, "It's a shame to waste food. It's a good thing that dog will eat anything. What was the matter with you — not hungry this morning?"

"I'm not sure," Dexter said, following Schuyler out of the kitchen.

The other kids were moving out of the house and heading for classes. Dexter followed, and when he closed the front door, he pulled off the door handle. He didn't do it on purpose. He didn't really know how he did it. But he was convinced something funny was happening to him.

Back in the kitchen, something funny was also happening to Brutus. His enemy, a huge dog, was at the window barking at him, but little Brutus wasn't showing his usual signs of fear. He had just tasted his cereal, and clouds of smoke were billowing out of his nostrils. Then he turned to the window and growled.

The huge dog sensed the turn of events about to take place. As Brutus charged out of the room running for the front door, the huge dog started his retreat.

Little Brutus knocked down the front door. Then, roaring like a lion, he charged down the street in pursuit of his enemy. The commotion caused Dexter, Debbie, and other students to turn. They laughed at the sight of the little dog chasing the big dog. It was a funny scene to all of them, except Dexter. He was beginning to put things together. That cereal!

A pebble in Dexter's shoe took his mind off the dog and off the cereal they had both eaten. Reaching for his shoe, he leaned on a nearby lamppost for balance. Then as the other students gasped, Dexter saw that he had bent the lamppost and began to realize what was happening.

Dexter again started up the street. By now he had a crowd following him. A basketball from a nearby court rolled up to Dexter's feet. He picked it up. He *knew* now, and he wanted to show off a little. Winking at Debbie, he dribbled toward the basket as the young players and the crowd watched.

Dexter leaped high into the air and dunked the ball! He had expected to dunk it, but he didn't expect to pull down the entire backboard! He wonderingly felt his arm, then started back down the street the way he had come.

"Hey, Dexter! You're going the wrong way," Debbie called after him.

"No, I'm not," Dexter called back, and Debbie and the amazed crowd turned to follow him.

Dexter got as far as Schuyler's car. Schuyler was under the back end of it, fixing something. Dexter turned for a moment to the crowd following him, then strutted over to the car and lifted its rear end up to his shoulders.

Schuyler was shocked — so shocked that he couldn't even think about the oil dripping in his face.

"Come on, genius," Dexter said, grinning at him. "We have work to do."

The first thing Dexter wanted to do was eat some more cereal. After that, he and Schuyler and the other students could start their search for Professor Quigley. They were going to pay a call on Dean Higgins.

Had they decided to go to the Dean first, they would have found Quigley right away. He was waiting in Higgins' outer office. Inside, Higgins was yelling at a fat student named Elmer.

"Elmer, you have to stop eating in class," Higgins warned.

"I can't help it," Elmer explained. "I get hungry once in a while."

Dexter leaps *high* into the air and dunks the ball!

"Once in a while?" Higgins repeated, glancing through a stack of reports on Elmer. "I have reports here from your first, third, fourth, and seventh periods, all complaining about your eating. All that bag-rattling and cracker-crunching when people are trying to study! And that's not the half of it. The janitors are complaining about large cake crumbs all over every room where you have classes. Now, Elmer, you're going to have to stop this. Janitors are hard to get."

Higgins paused, waiting for his message to sink into Elmer's head. He didn't hear the noise in his outer office, where the students had found Quigley and were explaining what had happened to Dexter.

"Consider this a final warning, Elmer," Higgins said. "I don't care what you do outside of class, but *in* class, no more jellybeans, no more cake, no more cookies — no more food, period!"

"Guess what? Schuyler said, bursting into the Dean's office, followed by the other students who were dragging Professor Quigley along with them.

"Guess nothing!" Higgins roared. "What do you mean crashing into my office while I'm reprimanding a student?"

"Sorry, we didn't mean to interrupt," Schuyler apologized, "but something has happened to Dexter."

"Something's always happening to Dexter. That's no excuse," Higgins said. Then he noticed Quigley. "Quigley, what are you doing here?"

Before Quigley could answer, Schuyler said,

"Listen, Dexter got strong. I mean really strong! Professor Quigley's ideas on that vitamin formula really worked!"

"Are you still talking about the formula you used on that so-called cow?" Higgins asked.

"Yes, sir," Schuyler said. "That's it."

"That's *it*, all right!" Higgins walked over to the door and threw it open. "All of you, out of here, right now! And I mean now!"

"Wait!" Schuyler called. "Look!"

They all looked at Dexter. He was lifting Elmer, chair and all, over his head with his right hand, and he was grinning while doing it.

"Good heavens!" Higgins was amazed.

"And that's only with his right hand," Schuyler said excitedly. "Show him what you can do with your left, Dex."

Holding Elmer aloft, Dexter bent and allowed Schuyler to step into the palm of his left hand. Then he lifted his friend overhead.

"See what I mean?" Schuyler called down to Higgins.

Higgins moved back to his desk, almost dizzy from Dexter's performance. Then Elmer called, "Hey, lemme down, will you?"

"Yes," Higgins agreed. "Please put him down before he breaks something."

Dexter put Elmer and Schuyler back on the floor, while Higgins seated himself at his desk. Then he said to Dexter, "Now tell me. How did this all happen?"

Taking out the box of cereal, Dexter said, "I don't know, really. I just ate some of Schuyler's cereal and all of a sudden I got strong."

"Let me see that box of cereal," said Higgins,

Dexter lifts fat Elmer, chair and all, in one hand and supports Schuyler in the palm of his other hand. Crumply Crunch *is* the cereal of champions!

taking the box from Dexter's hand and examining it. "You know, this is the same stuff I eat every morning and I never got strong."

Schuyler laughed. "Of course not," he said. "It's not the cereal that made him strong. It was my...I mean, Professor Quigley's and my formula. Plain old cereal wouldn't do anything like what happened to Dexter, no matter what those companies say."

"No, it wouldn't," Higgins agreed.

For a moment, Dean Higgins seemed to be staring off into space. In truth, he was thinking, but it was something the students weren't used to seeing him do. Finally, Dexter said, "Dean Higgins, what's the matter?"

"Oh, nothing, nothing at all," the Dean answered. "But would you young people mind leaving the room for a moment? I'd like to talk to Professor Quigley."

All the students started out the door and Dexter asked, "Do you mean he's still working here?"

"Of course he's still working here," Higgins said. "Why wouldn't he be? I don't know where you kids get some of the crazy ideas that pop into your heads."

After the door was closed, Higgins came back to his desk. He smiled at Quigley. Then he said, almost in a whisper, "Quigley, do you realize what we have here?"

The Strongest Man in the World

CHAPTER FOUR

Did Quigley realize what they had? Of course he realized. Without hesitation he said, "It seems like we have a pretty amazing scientific discovery."

"It's more than that," Higgins corrected. "We having something that will get this school out of hock forever." Then he picked up the cereal box. "Quigley," he said, "can you guess what a cereal company would give to have a strength formula like this in their cereal?"

"Well, no," Quigley answered. "I never really thought about it."

"Well, think about it," Higgins said. "It can mean new buildings, a new lab, and money for all kinds of experiments for the betterment and enrichment of mankind."

Quigley was catching on. "And besides," he said, "if something doesn't happen pretty soon around here, you're going to lose your job."

"That's not the point," Higgins said. Then he pressed the intercom on his desk and said to his secretary, "Mercedes, please get me the President of the Crumply Crunch Cereal Company at Coyote Corners, Kern County, Connecticut.

Tell her I want to see her immediately...just me."

"What about the boys?" Quigley asked as Higgins picked up his phone. "They were the ones that did it."

Higgins held his hand over the phone and said, "Quigley, I'm not taking any of those clowns up there. This is very important business and it should be handled by a very important man."

The President of the Crumply Crunch Cereal Company, Mrs. Harriet Crumply, wasn't too enthusiastic about Dean Higgins and the strength formula he wanted to demonstrate to her. Finally, though, she agreed to allow the Dean to make a presentation of the formula at the next regular meeting of the company's Board of Directors.

Higgins was delighted. He met with Quigley and the students to work out a plan. I'll have to take a box of the cereal with me," Higgins told them. "And for special effects, I'll have to take a dumbbell with me."

"I'll go," Dexter said hopefully.

Dexter's hopes quickly disappeared when he realized what Higgins wanted was a barbell. It was borrowed from the gym.

When the time came, Higgins went off excited and confident; Quigley and the students were also excited, though not as confident. Still, the good wishes of all went out to Higgins. His success was going to mean a lot to Medfield.

Crumply Crunch's Board members were really bored members, Higgins thought, as he set up the mat and barbell in the space he had cleared in the Board Room. They were milling around, talking to one another, and not a one of them seemed even slightly interested in him. Finally, he pulled one member over to the barbell and showed him how heavy it was.

"I see what you mean," the Board member said, after he hurt his back attempting to lift the barbell. "That's no light weight."

On the other side of the room, Harry, Mrs. Crumply's nephew, said to another Board member, "Can you imagine the boss falling for a strength demonstration from that weird looking character? She's over the hill, I guess. She should step down and let a younger person run things."

"That person wouldn't happen to be you, would it, Harry?" the other Board member asked.

Harry shrugged. "Who else?" he asked, and then moved to join the rest of the Board who were seating themselves.

When everyone in the room was seated, including Dean Higgins, a Board member said, "Gentlemen, as you know, the Chairman of the Board hasn't arrived yet. However, I would like to welcome Dean Higgins and ask him to be patient with us for a few minutes."

Nodding graciously, Higgins said, "Thank you, gentlemen. I assure you my time is your time."

"Yes, well, unfortunately our time is not yours," Harry Crumply said, looking at his watch. "It is approximately two minutes past one. I humbly suggest you demonstrate what-

25

ever this thing is you're going to demonstrate. Then we can get on with the real business of this meeting.

"But we can't start without the Chairman," one Board member said.

"We can't?" Harry repeated. "As Senior Vice President and second in command, I will say when we can start."

For a moment, there was a flurry of whispers around the table. Then the door burst open, and a regal, dynamic looking woman came striding into the room. It was Harriet Crumply, the President and Chairman of the Board.

"Trying to start without me again, Harry?" she asked her nephew.

"Who, me?" Harry fumbled. "Oh, no, of course not. You know I wouldn't do anything like that, Aunt Harriet, I mean, Mrs. Crumply."

"Aunt Harriet will be fine," she answered, allowing a few Board members to help her into her seat. "But remember, just because you're a relative, that doesn't mean I can't fire you. And that goes for the rest of you, too."

The Board members became uneasy after Aunt Harriet's remark, especially when she followed it by smiling around the table at them. Then she said, "Now will the Secretary tell us what's first on the agenda?"

"Yes, Aunt Harriet," a young man said, motioning in Higgins' direction. "This is Dean Higgins. He's the one that claims to have that strength formula."

"Oh, yes, I talked to you on the telephone," Aunt Harriet said. "You're the funny little man from that funny little school downstate."

"I guess I am," Higgins answered.

"And you want to demonstrate your strength formula for us."

Standing, Higgins said proudly, "Madam, that is precisely why I'm here."

Then Higgins whipped off his overcoat. Underneath it, he was wearing an old-fashioned Medfield sweat outfit which looked very much like a pair of long johns.

"Oh, my!" Aunt Harriet said, surprised by his appearance.

"This is my old gym outfit," Higgins explained. "We weren't very fussy in those days."

"Well, it's kind of cute," Aunt Harriet said. "Now you go ahead."

Higgins seated himself at the table and poured some cereal into a bowl and added milk. Almost immediately, the cereal began to snap, crackle, and pop, and the Board members stared at it. Then Higgins lifted a spoonful of the cereal up to his mouth and started to eat it. As he chewed, puffs of smoke poured from his nostrils and fogged his glasses. He lifted them off and threw them aside. Then he pounded his chest and yelled, "*Ai-ee!*"

Aunt Harriet's mouth was hanging open. "Excuse me," Higgins said. "That was a throwback I didn't think was in me. Now, with your permission, I shall begin with a little weight lifting."

"Splendid," Aunt Harriet said. "You go right ahead."

Higgins smiled and walked over to the barbell. Then he flipped the barbell into the air and caught it with one hand and lifted it overhead.

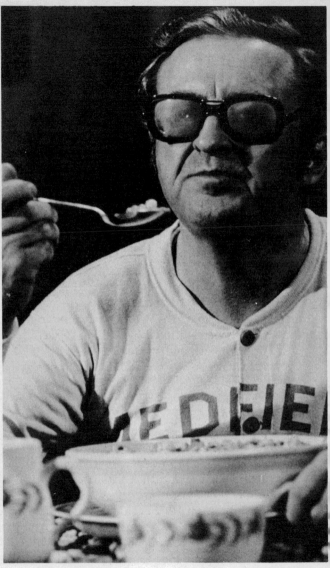

Who turned out the lights? As Dean Higgins chews a spoonful of cereal, puffs of smoke pour from his nostrils and fog his glasses.

"Bravo!" cried Aunt Harriet, joining the other Board members in wild applause.

Higgins loved the attention he was getting. It encouraged him to perform, and perform he did. First, he twirled the barbell like a baton. Then, acting like a trained seal, he balanced the weight on his nose and walked around the room. Finally, he put down the barbell and bowed to his audience. The Board members stood and cheered, all except Harry.

Higgins walked to where Harry was seated. Spotting a paperweight on the table in front of Harry, he picked it up and walked to the center section of the table. Then he raised his arm and crushed the paperweight in his hand!

The cheers started again, and Aunt Harriet called, "Bravo! Bravo!"

Higgins smiled and walked over to her. Then he lifted her, chair and all, over his head. Again, the Board members applauded wildly, as Higgins set Aunt Harriet back on the floor.

Bowing once more and smiling, Higgins raised his hands and said, "That's not all, folks, that's not all. You haven't seen anything yet."

Seconds later, Higgins leaped onto the table. From there, he caught hold of one of the light fixtures above the table and began to swing from one light to the other like a trapeze artist. After one mighty final swing, he did a mid-air flip and landed on his feet at the center of the table.

At this point, the Board members might well have concluded that Higgins' cereal was all that he claimed it to be. However, some of the formula seemed to have gone to Higgins' head. He backward-flipped himself off the table. Then he gave the table a terrifying karate chop and yelled, "*Ay Yah!*"

The table trembled under the blow. Then it shook! Then a crack appeared in the end of it and moved down the table slowly. Fear showed on the Board members' faces, as they watched the table shake once more and collapse.

After the table collapsed, the Board members relaxed and again cheered Higgins and called out for more feats of strength.

If there was any good sense left in Higgins, the cheers destroyed it. He whirled around and moved to a building pillar. Then he shook it and plaster began falling. It seemed as if the building, like the table, was about to collapse.

"Stop, Dean Higgins!" Aunt Harriet cried. "Please, stop!"

Some Board members and Aunt Harriet raced over to Higgins and grabbed him, pleading with him to stop.

"Excuse me," Higgins finally said. "I guess I got carried away."

It was time to talk business, and Aunt Harriet and the Board members returned to the now-demolished table. "Now tell me, Dean Higgins, how long does this strength stay with you?" Aunt Harriet asked.

"Well, we don't know exactly," Higgins explained. "It depends on the person and the amount of formula used. But I would say that the duration of the strength is definitely limited."

This alarmed Aunt Harriet, but one Board member said quickly, "All the better, Aunt Harriet. If a person were to lose his strength, he

Dean Higgins proves to be an accomplished trapeze artist
as he gracefully swings from chandelier to chandelier.

would have to eat more cereal to regain it. Why, we could sell cereal morning, noon, and night."

The idea thrilled Aunt Harriet. She settled into her chair and said, "Gentlemen, after all these years of having, as one might say, 'our noses rubbed in it,' by Krinkle Krunch Cereal, we will now be number one!"

The Board members responded with wild enthusiasm, while Aunt Harriet looked around on the floor for the telephone that had been knocked down with the table. When she found the phone, the Board members settled down in their chairs and she said, "Dean Higgins, do you have a weight-lifting team?"

"No," Higgins said, "we don't exactly have the personnel for that sport."

"Good," Aunt Harriet said, pressing her intercom button. "Stanley, I would like to speak to Mr. Kirkwood Krinkle of the Krinkle Krunch Cereal Company at Katastrophe Creek, Catspaw County, Connecticut."

The Board members were shocked. They didn't trust Krinkle — he was the enemy. Harry stood up and said, "What are you doing, talking to Krinkle?"

"Just wait and see," Aunt Harriet answered calmly.

Krinkle was meeting with his Board when the call came. He couldn't believe his ears — a challenge from Harriet Crumply.

"A weight-lifting contest between State and Medfield," Krinkle repeated into the phone. "We were, I mean State was national champion last year. I guess you know I went there."

"Everyone knows that," Aunt Harriet said.

"What is the point of all this?" Krinkle asked.

"I am proposing that in the interest of sports — and the cereal business, of course — a much-publicized match be held between State and Medfield, and that your company support State and mine support Medfield. In this way, the public will be able to determine which is the number one weight-lifting team in America, and perhaps which is the number one cereal company."

"We are the number one cereal company already," Krinkle said. "Remember, Harriet?"

"Oh, I remember," Aunt Harriet said sarcastically. "And I can understand your fear about losing to us."

"Nonsense!" Krinkle roared. "Krinkle Krunch is always ready for competition. I'll notify the papers immediately. It's a wonderful idea, Harriet, just wonderful. Thanks for calling."

Krinkle put down the receiver and turned to his Board. "Medfield versus State," he said, laughing. "What a joke! We'll murder them! Gentlemen, this weight-lifting match will forever destroy the reputation of Medfield College and with it the reputation of Aunt Harriet Crumply and that crummy Crumply Crunch Cereal of hers!"

Back at the Crumply Board Room, there was much excitement. All the Board members cheered Aunt Harriet's plan — all except Harry. For some unexplained reason, he seemed unhappy.

"You'll have to supply a small, under-nourished, puny team," Aunt Harriet told Higgins, "and a ton of your formula."

"An undernourished, puny team is no trouble," Higgins said. "But a *ton* of formula?"

"Yes, and after your team is seen on nation-wide television defeating State, the demand for our cereal will be overwhelming," Aunt Harriet explained. "And, of course, your school will be amply rewarded."

"Rewarded?" Higgins said. "I think we'll be able to deliver a ton without any trouble. In fact, I'm sure of it."

"Aunt Harriet," one Board member said, "don't you think you should remind Dean Higgins about spies?"

"Spies?" Higgins repeated.

"Yes, industrial spies, Dean Higgins," Aunt Harriet said. "There's no length to which Krinkle Krunch won't go to discover our plans."

"Well, I can assure you that this project will be kept top secret," Higgins promised. "I'll have the lab placed under top security. You won't have to worry about spies."

"Good," Aunt Harriet said. "Naturally, we employ a few spies of our own, but that other company has them everywhere. We just don't know who they are."

Though it went unnoticed, one Board member cheerfully agreed with Aunt Harriet's thoughts about spies. He was one of them, and he was her nephew Harry. Smiling and puffing on his cigar, he blew a smoke ring and wished the meeting were over.

The Strongest Man In the World

CHAPTER FIVE

That same night, a man climbed out of his limousine on an almost deserted road. For a second, he looked around. Then he stepped into a phone booth and carefully dialed a familiar number.

A phone rang in another part of the same state. The man in the booth waiting for the call picked up the receiver. "This is me," he said.

"This is me," Harry answered.

"Good. Were you followed?" the man asked.

Harry looked again. "I don't think so," he said.

"Well, what is it, Harry?"

"You're in trouble, Krinkle."

Kirkwood Krinkle of the Krinkle Krunch Cereal Company glanced outside the phone booth, wondering what Harry was talking about. Then he said, "What kind of trouble?"

"The weight-lifting match," Harry said. "Withdraw."

"Withdraw!" Krinkle repeated. "You must be kidding. State has the greatest weight-lifting team in the country. Why, we'll wipe Medfield off the map."

"She's sandbagging you, Krinkle," Harry warned.

"Sandbagging me?"

"Yeah," Harry said. "That Medfield bunch came up with a strength formula to put in Aunt Harriet's cereal that will literally knock your number one out. I'm telling you to withdraw."

"I can't withdraw," Krinkle said. "I've already had a press conference today and announced the whole thing. In fact, I even bragged a little."

"Then you're going to be number two," Harry warned. "I saw a demonstration of how that formula works and believe me, Medfield's going to slaughter State."

Harry's words angered Krinkle. "Medfield's not going to slaughter State and Krinkle Krunch will never be number two, Harry," he said. "I'm counting on you to get that formula. It's worth a hundred thousand dollars to me."

"It's worth a lot more than that," Harry said.

"Okay," Krinkle said quickly. "A hundred and fifty."

"One hundred and fifty's okay for me," Harry answered, "but this is a big job, and I'll need some help."

"Fifty more for the help," Krinkle said, "but for heaven's sake, get some good people."

"Don't worry, Mr. Krinkle," Harry said cheerfully. "I think I have the right party in mind — exactly the right party."

Then Harry hung up the phone. Both men waited a moment. Then they stepped from their respective phone booths and walked to their limousines. Seconds later, the two chauffeur-driven limousines raced off into the night. In one, a man was thinking about the money he had just agreed to spend. In the other, a man was thinking about spending the money he had just agreed to take.

Harry didn't have any trouble finding the party he had in mind. His name was Arno, and he was just ending a period of residence in State Prison.

The prison gates swung open for Arno and his pal Cookie the next day. Arno was wearing his usual suavely-tailored gray suit. "Good-bye," he said to the gate guard. "It's always a pleasure to visit you. Just so it's not for too long."

"Come anytime, Mr. Arno," the guard said, smiling. "Our house is your house."

Arno laughed. "Thank you," he called back to the guard.

"What did he mean?" Cookie said, as the gates closed. "It's not my house. I never want to go back to that joint again."

"He's only putting you on, stupid," Arno explained. "Besides, we won't have to go back there again if you don't louse up anymore."

Cookie looked puzzled. "Boss," he said, "how come you always blame *me* when we get into predicaments?"

Arno realized the question called for an explanation. "Because," he said, "it's your stupidity that gets us into these predicaments, that's why."

Satisfied, Cookie shook his head. Then they both noticed Harry getting out of his limousine. "It's Harry," Arno said. "It's sure nice of him to be here to greet us."

Harry not only greeted them. He offered a ride into town. The two men accepted, and Arno

Arno and Cookie say good-bye to State Prison. "Come any-time, Mr. Arno," the guard says, smiling. "Our house is your house."

said, "How's life been treating you, Harry?"

"Couldn't be better," Harry said proudly. "This chauffeured limousine, a penthouse downtown, everything is great. How about you?"

Arno looked back at the prison through the limousine's rear window. "As you might guess, I've had a temporary setback," he said, "but don't worry about that. I'll be right back on top before I know it."

Harry smiled. "I know you will," he said. "As a matter of fact, that's just what I had in mind."

"Okay," Arno said. "What's the deal?"

Looking at Cookie, Harry said, "Is he okay?"

"Sure," Arno answered. "He's kind of stupid, but he's okay."

"What are you talking that way again for?" Cookie said to Arno. "You keep that kind of talk up, and you're going to cause me to lose my confidence."

Harry and Arno laughed. Then they settled down to business. Harry explained about the Medfield strength formula and the security men that would be at the school to protect the secret of the formula from leaking out. It wasn't going to be easy, Harry explained, but there was a lot of money in the deal for Arno and Cookie.

"Don't worry," Arno told Harry, as the limousine pulled up to the boarding house where he and Cookie planned to stay. "Getting that formula is going to be easy as pie."

After the limousine pulled away, Cookie said, "What kind of pie, Arno? I thought he said cereal."

"Easy as pie is just an expression, stupid,"

Arno answered. "It means *very easy*. In fact, this thing is going to be so easy that I'm going to let you go out to Medfield tomorrow afternoon and figure the whole thing out for us."

"Me? Figure the whole thing out for us? Cookie mumbled to himself, following Arno into the boarding house. Then he smiled and said, "You're right, Arno. It sounds like it's going to be simple."

The Strongest Man In the World

CHAPTER SIX

As night replaced the next day at Medfield College, two workmen were just putting the finishing touches on a new cement walk in front of the College's administration building. They were anxious to finish and go home — too anxious to notice the two men hiding in a clump of bushes a few feet away from them.

Waiting for the workmen to leave wasn't helping Arno's nerves. From behind the bushes, he looked up at the scaffold hanging from the top of the administration building and terror showed on his face.

"Don't worry," Cookie whispered to him. "As soon as those guys get into their cement truck and leave, we go around the back and get up on the roof. Then we go down the scaffold and get into the lab. The formula's right there."

"I don't like this scaffold business," Arno answered.

"I cased the joint this afternoon, boss," Cookie whispered to him. "The corridors are loaded with security cops. It's the window or nothing, so we have to use the scaffold."

"All right," Arno said, "but letting you case the joint is probably the biggest mistake I ever made."

Cookie didn't answer. He was watching the workmen set down a "Caution Wet Cement" sign. Seconds later he said, "Okay, the truck's leaving. Follow me."

Cookie raced off before Arno could answer. Still very nervous, Arno raced after him, calling, "Wait for me!"

By the time the two men reached the top of the administration building, a strong wind was beating against them. "You know," Arno said, "it's windier up here than it is down there."

"That's because it's higher up here than it is down there," Cookie explained, as he climbed over a ledge and got ready to drop down on the scaffold.

Cookie dropped down easily. Then he said to Arno, "Come on."

Arno was very shaky. He slowly eased his body down, allowing Cookie to guide his movements. Finally, when Arno's feet were almost touching the scaffold, Cookie said, "Perfect."

Arno's feet and full weight hit the scaffolding, and it pulled away from the wall. In desperation, Arno leaned stiffly against the wall, causing the scaffold to move further away from it. He looked down and saw the ground far below him. "Oh, no, I'm going to die," he cried.

To keep himself from falling, Cookie, too, was forced to lean against the building. He was frightened, but he took a deep breath and said, "Boss, you're not going to die. Maybe you've gone a little bit nuts, but you're not going to die. Now all you have to do is let go of the wall and we'll be okay."

Arno was frozen with fear. "I can't let go," he cried.

Cookie grabbed Arno's arm. They struggled, and as Arno fought back, he let go of the wall. When he did, the scaffold flew back at the wall and slammed into it. The crash almost sent both men off the edge, and they grabbed each other for safety.

"You're violent," Cookie told Arno.

"And you're an idiot," Arno answered. "What are you trying to do, kill me?"

Feeling confident again, Cookie walked to the other end of the scaffold and said, "The worst part's over now, boss. The rest is a cinch. All we have to do is work the ropes right and we're in that room."

"And you know how to work the ropes?" Arno said doubtfully.

"Sure," Cookie answered. "I worked them all by myself today in a phony window-washing job. With you helping me, it ought to be easy. All we have to do is release the rope down to the next notch and we'll go down nice and easy."

The two men started to work at opposite ends of the scaffold. As each man released his side, the scaffold began to move evenly down the side of the building.

"See, there's nothing to it," Cookie said, turning to Arno and allowing his attention to drift away from the rope running through his hand.

"Yeah," Arno agreed, "this does work pretty good."

"Sure it does," Cookie said. "I told you I

had it all figured out. You know, boss, you froze over nothing. That's not good for your heart. You have to learn to trust other people to figure things out sometime."

"People like you?" Arno said.

Unfortunately, while Cookie was talking, a knot was forming in the pulley, and before he could answer, his side of the platform jerked to a sudden stop. Arno's side continued downward, and Arno screamed in horror. Then he fell to his hands and knees.

The platform's uneven angle caused Cookie to slide to Arno's end and knock into him. The crash pushed Arno off the scaffold, and he grabbed the rope to save his life. Then he and Cookie had a wild struggle, before Cookie was able to pull him back onto the platform.

"Well, I got you, boss," Cookie said. "But I don't blame you for being scared. I thought you were a goner for a while there."

Shaking his head, Arno said, "You are an idiot."

"Boss, it wasn't me," Cookie said, climbing to his feet. "It was a knot in the rope. I'm going to fix it."

Cookie probably did intend to fix things, but it clearly wasn't his night. Seconds later a plank slid out of the platform, and Arno was again hanging on for dear life. And to add to his troubles, a bucket of soapy water had overturned and was flowing into his face.

After much struggling and some sudden stops of the scaffold, the two men found themselves in front of the lab window. As they climbed

Hang in there, Boss! A falling board has tripped Arno. If he doesn't hold on to the scaffold, he'll never get that secret formula.

through the window, Arno said, "Going back, we take the stairs."

"But the halls are loaded with security guys," Cookie protested.

"I'll take my chances with those security guys," Arno said. "I'm not getting back on that scaffold with you."

"Boss, I know how to work the ropes now," Cookie said. "Honest, I do."

"I don't want to hear any more about those ropes," Arno cautioned. "Let's get that formula and be quick about it."

"No problem," Cookie answered, motioning to a desk. "It should be over here somewhere. The kid was working at this desk today."

When Cookie reached the desk, he opened the drawer, and threw a light from his flashlight over it. It was empty. "That's funny," Cookie announced.

"What's funny about it?" Arno asked angrily. "You drag me up here in the middle of the night and almost get me killed on that stupid scaffold and all you can say is — 'that's funny'? Well, it's not funny to me."

"It's got to be around here somewhere," Cookie said apologetically. "I could have sworn I saw him put it in this desk. I was washing the window. It sure is funny."

"Will you quit saying funny?" Arno pleaded. "And hurry up and find the formula. It's worth fifty thousand bucks to us."

They quickly and quietly searched through some nearby desks. Then the quiet was broken by a sound — a droning sound. "What's that?" Arno whispered.

Cookie listened for a moment. Then he said, "It sounds like somebody snoring to me."

Cookie was right. Leaning back in a chair against the other side of the lab door was a security guard. He was sound asleep.

"You are ridiculous," Arno answered, staring up at the ceiling. "They may have this joint bugged. They're probably picking up everything we say. In fact, I'm sure that's it. We'd better get out of here in a hurry — and quietly."

As Arno headed for the lab door, Cookie pleaded, "Boss, not out the door. The place is crawling with guards."

Arno stopped for a moment. "Cookie," he said, "I've taken over. We do it my way now. You're following me from now on. Now let's go."

"Whatever you say, boss," Cookie answered, shrugging his shoulders and moving toward the door.

Arno had taken over, all right, and his first act was almost his last move. He unlocked the door and pulled it open. A chair and a sleeping security guard landed at Arno's and Cookie's feet. Without speaking to each other, they quickly lifted the chair and guard upright and set the chair back down in the corridor.

The security guard's eyes opened wide, just as Arno and Cookie slammed the door shut behind him. Then he blew his whistle.

Inside the lab, Arno locked the door. Then he and Cookie raced for the window.

More guards had arrived outside the door. They were trying to break it down. Whistles were screaming, and as the lab door began to break into splinters, Arno hurried over to the scaffold ropes and said to Cookie, "I'll handle the ropes this time."

After all the trouble they had getting to the lab, Arno wasn't going to let Cookie pull anything else. So Arno pulled something — a rope, and the entire scaffold gave way. And Arno and his partner sailed off, landing face down in the wet cement in front of the administration building.

By the time the security guards reached the lab window, Arno and Cookie were gone. The guards weren't totally disappointed though. Arno and Cookie had left perfect impressions of themselves in the cement.

The Strongest Man In the World
CHAPTER SEVEN

Harry was mad. The morning newspaper carried a photo of some fine cement likenesses of Arno and Cookie. Security was doubled at Medfield, and time was running out for Harry.

Fortunately, as the three of them met, a new idea came into Arno's head. "I know a certain Chinese gentleman who can be a great help in a case like this," he told Harry. "In fact, I think we'll be able to take care of everything tonight."

Harry didn't have time to stick around the boarding house, but he warned Arno, "I'm beginning to lose my confidence in you, Arno. You had better get the formula tonight."

"Don't worry," Arno told him. "Cookie will get started on it right now."

After Harry left, Cookie said, "I guess I'd better get started."

"On what?" Arno asked.

"Oh, that's right," Cookie said, sitting down again. "On what?"

When Arno started explaining, it all seemed very simple. It always did.

By nightfall, the two men had completed every step in Arno's new plan. They were seated in Arno's limousine, waiting. Cookie was seated in front with a shopping bag beside him. Arno was seated in back with the students' dog, Brutus, on his lap.

While Arno struggled to hold the dog's mouth shut, Cookie asked, "Are you sure this Schuyler is going to come looking for the dog?"

"Here he comes now," Arno said, motioning Cookie to move the car down the street to Schuyler, who was searching for little Brutus.

When the car stopped, Arno hopped out and carried the dog over to Schuyler. Then he set it on the ground, and the little dog barked cheerfully and ran to his friend. At the same time, Cookie sneaked around the other side of the car. In his hand, he held the shopping bag.

"Gee, thanks a lot," Schuyler said to Arno. "Where did you find him?"

"Oh, he was just wandering a few blocks down," Arno lied. "We picked him up and saw the address on his collar. We were just taking him there when we saw you. You seemed to be looking for a dog, so we stopped."

Schuyler was so happy he didn't see Cookie sneaking up behind him. "Well, it was sure nice of you," Schuyler told Arno. "You know, I recognized you right away, Mr. Arno. I didn't even know you were out of prison, but I don't care what anyone says about you. Anyone who is so thoughtful about dogs sure is a friend of mine."

"Think nothing of it, kid," Arno answered, just as Cookie pulled the shopping bag over Schuyler's head and pinned his arms.

Then Arno and Cookie quickly pushed Schuyler into the back seat of the limousine. Brutus started barking and biting at Arno's feet, but Arno kicked the little dog away and said, "Get out of here, you mutt."

Cookie started the engine, and the sleek limousine pulled away from the curb. Its destination was Ah Fong's Chinese Restaurant. There a group of Chinese businessmen were entertaining Medfield's Police Chief Blair at a dinner, but Arno and Cookie had no intention of seeing the Chief. Their business was in the restaurant's back room.

At the restaurant, Chief Blair had just started his speech when Schuyler was carried into the back room and tied down. The Chief didn't know that Dean Higgins was looking for him, wanting to report the kidnapping of his most important student. And the Chief had no reason to know that the student was in the restaurant. The Chief was happy. The businessmen were applauding his comments.

"You have to believe me," Schuyler pleaded with Cookie. "I don't know where the formula is, and I don't know what's in the formula."

"Boss," Cookie pleaded with Arno, "I hate to do it, but I have to get rough with this kid. Just give me five minutes alone and I'll find out. Five minutes is all I need, boss. It always works."

While all this pleading was going on, Ah Fong had entered the back room. "Honorable sir, I admire your enthusiasm," he said to Cookie. "But this boy can never tell you what is in the formula because he thinks he doesn't know."

"How do you know?" Cookie asked.

"I know," Ah Fong said confidently.

"See, he knows," Arno told Cookie. "Now you shut up!"

"In order to find truth," Ah Fong continued, "I must put boy in deep sleep. Then he will tell us all he knows."

"He's got to be kidding!" Cookie commented.

"Be patient, my son," Ah Fong answered. Then he walked over to the side door and disappeared behind a curtain.

Cookie turned to Arno and said angrily, "My son? Where does he get off calling me his son!"

"Maybe he likes you," Arno said.

"Well, I don't like him," Cookie answered. "He makes me feel funny—like maybe I'm not as smart as he is, or something."

"He does?" Arno said, holding back a grin. "I wonder why."

Before Cookie could respond, Ah Fong returned, followed by an assistant carrying a tray covered with acupuncture equipment.

"Now what's he going to do?" Cookie asked.

"With your permission," Ah Fong said to Arno, "I will do what you Americans call brainwash."

"Brainwash!" Cookie repeated. "I don't like this hocus-pocus stuff, boss. Why don't we go back to the old-fashioned way and belt the kid around a little."

"Will you be quiet!" Arno warned. "I'm paying Fong to do this."

Schuyler watched as Ah Fong took a long needle from the tray. The needle frightened him.

"Have no fear," Ah Fong said. "I put you in hypnotic trance. It will cause deep sleep—make you feel very happy."

"What's with the needle?" Cookie asked.

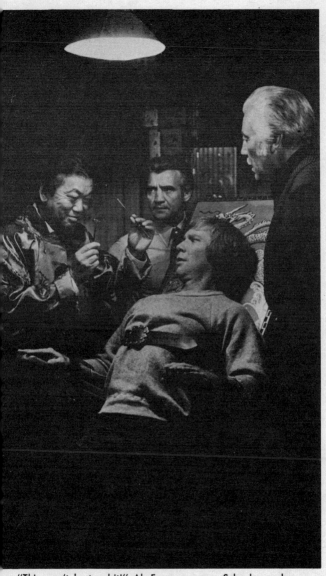

"This won't hurt a bit!" Ah Fong reassures Schuyler as he uses acupuncture, a painless form of brainwashing, to get the secret formula.

"I must use acupuncture," Ah Fong explained. "It is fashionable today among modern Chinese."

Arno, Cookie, and Schuyler watched silently as Ah Fong pointed a needle over Schuyler's head. Then he asked for a mallet. "This won't hurt," he told Schuyler, who wanted to believe him.

Then Ah Fong hit the top of the needle with a tiny mallet, and the needle went into Schuyler's head. Almost immediately, a silly grin settled on Schuyler's face.

"See, the patient is happy," Ah Fong said. "You are tired, my son. Your eyes are heavy. You will sleep. You will be happy. You will go into a deep, deep, deep sleep."

Elbowing Cookie, Arno said, "He's talking to the kid, stupid."

Cookie quickly came out of it.

"When I snap my fingers," Ah Fong continued, "you will open your eyes and answer my questions, though you will still be asleep."

Then Ah Fong snapped his fingers and Schuyler's eyes opened wide.

In amazement, Cookie said, "Isn't that peachy, boss?"

Arno didn't answer. He, too, was amazed!

"Remember, we are friends," Ah Fong told Schuyler. "You shall tell us everything you know. Everything—right from the beginning."

A blank stare came over Schuyler's face and he said, "Right from the beginning? Oh, yes, now I remember. Mary had a little lamb, her fleece was white as snow."

"What?" Arno asked, trying to find some hidden meaning in Schuyler's words.

"Not quite that far back," Ah Fong said. "Tell us about the formula. Do you remember what you put in your strength formula?"

Schuyler paused, and as Arno quickly pulled a pad and pencil from his pocket, Ah Fong said, "Proceed, please."

"Unit consistency," Schuyler mumbled, "six hundred decigrams thiamine....Seven hundred centigrams calcium pentathemate....Nine hundred milligrams niacin....Four hundred fifty centigrams pyridoxine....Five hundred milligrams pyradexamine....On a sesame seed bun...."

Schuyler slipped back into a deep sleep, and Arno asked, "What was that?"

"On a sesame seed bun," Ah Fong answered.

"There's got to be more," Arno said nervously.

"Oh," Cookie said, "you mean 'two all-beef patties, pickles, onions, and...' there's more, but I never get it right, boss. "

"Shut up, you dummy," Arno answered. "What do you think, Ah Fong?"

"Perhaps, special sauce," Ah Fong said, smiling. Then he turned to his assistant and said, "Another needle, please."

In the meantime, Police Chief Blair had just completed his speech, and he was working his way to the front door of the restaurant, stopping briefly along the way to shake hands and chat briefly with his hosts. Outside, his car was waiting, surrounded by photographers and reporters.

The reporters probably would have been much more interested in what was going on in the back room, and the photographers would have loved to get some photos of Schuyler, because he now had two long needles sticking out of his forehead.

"Is there anything else, my son?" Ah Fong asked Schuyler.

"Oh, yes," Schuyler said, "I almost forgot. One piece of pizza."

This final bit of information surprised all three men. "I must admit," Ah Fong said, "that is most unusual ingredient for medical formula. However, ways of Western people are very strange at times."

"What else can you expect from that dopey kid?" Arno said. "He came up with a formula that's just crazy enough to work. Well, we'll get this off to Harry. He says that Krinkle Cereal guy is waiting for it."

"Wait a second, boss," Cookie cautioned. "We've got to take care of this kid. He can identify us."

"The young man will be unable to identify anyone," Ah Fong corrected. "He will remember only what I tell him to remember. He will do only what I want him to do."

"Good!" Arno said. "I trust you, Fong. Get the kid home as soon as possible and make sure he doesn't remember anything, but first give Cookie and me a minute to get out of here."

Fong watched Arno and Cookie go out the back door. Then he turned his attention to Schuyler. "My son, you will awake when I clap my hands," Ah Fong said. "When you do, you will remember nothing. You will not remember where you have been, nor what has happened to you. All you will know is that your little dog is home and that he is looking for you. He needs you. You must hurry to him. You must get home quickly. Take the first means of transportation you see. Do not worry about people. They will understand."

Ah Fong released Schuyler's bindings. Then he clapped his hands. Schuyler got up quickly and rushed out the door leading into the restaurant. Ah Fong smiled. His duties were ended.

Schuyler rushed through the restaurant. Outside, he came upon Police Chief Blair and a group of businessmen getting positioned for a photograph. "Oh, excuse me," Schuyler said, as he bumped into the Chief. "I have to go home to my dog. He is waiting for me."

Turning to a reporter, the Chief said, "His dog is waiting for him. Now there's a loyal young man."

The chief was about to find out just how loyal Schuyler was, because Schuyler's eyes settled on the Chief's car. In his mind, he heard Ah Fong's words: "You must get home quickly. Take the first means of transportation you see. Do not worry about people. They will understand."

Schuyler didn't hesitate. He jumped into the Chief's car, started it, and pulled away, around a group of police motor bikes.

When the Chief caught sight of his car pulling away, he flew into a rage. "Get that kid!" he screamed at the policemen on their bikes. "He has my car!"

The motor bikes started to pull out, and the Chief ran over and leaped on the rear end of one of the bikes. "After him!" he roared.

Just then, two small children passed the Chief and waved American flags at him. As the Chief straightened up and saluted, the bike pulled away, and the Chief went sailing off the bike into the street. Disgusted, he sat there, while the photographers snapped pictures of him.

Schuyler almost made it back to Medfield. The police captured him on the walk leading to the school, and Dean Higgins and Quigley followed them to the police station. After a quick session with a judge, bail was set for Schuyler, and Dean Higgins reluctantly paid it.

Outside the police station, Schuyler said, "Sorry about the bail money, Dean Higgins."

"Sorry has nothing to do with it," Higgins said. "You're paying me that one hundred dollars back."

"There's one thing I don't understand, Schuyler," Quigley said. "What were you doing in a Chinese restaurant?"

"I don't understand it either," Schuyler said. "I don't remember a thing."

"You didn't happen to talk to anyone, did you?" Quigley asked.

"I don't think so," Schuyler answered, puzzling over the night's events.

"He doesn't think so," Higgins repeated angrily.

"Think hard," Quigley said. "You didn't talk to anyone about anything important, did you?"

"Important?" Schuyler said, bewildered by the question.

"He means about the formula," Higgins said angrily.

"Oh, of course not," Schuyler said, laughing. "Don't worry about the formula. I got that all locked up here in my head."

Dean Higgins didn't bother to answer, but he was worried. He would have worried about anything locked up in Schuyler's head, but he didn't say so.

The Strongest Man in the World

CHAPTER EIGHT

Harry passed the formula along to Krinkle and collected the money for him and for Arno and Cookie. Krinkle was delighted by Harry's rapid success and passed the formula along to his chemists. "All I need is a bowlful for this afternoon," he told the chemists.

Then Krinkle got started on calling all his Board members for a special meeting. At the special meeting, he intended to give them a personal demonstration of the effects of the strength formula. He had made about half of his calls when his phone rang. It was one of his chemists. "We've got the slice of pizza and all the chemicals," the chemist said, "but we were wondering where we can get a sesame seed bun?"

"You fools," Krinkle said, "Why don't you try..."

Before he could finish his sentence, the chemist interrupted and said, "We tried it, boss, but they won't sell us a plain sesame seed bun."

"So get the two all-beef patties, special sauce, cheese, lettuce, too," Krinkle said. "And then take all that stuff off the bun."

"Good idea, boss," the chemist said, hanging up on Krinkle.

"Good idea," Krinkle repeated, smiling to himself. Then he set about making his remaining calls to the Board.

By mid-afternoon, the Board of Directors had assembled in Krinkle's Board Room. They watched as their leader poured some Krinkle Krunch into a bowl. Then he poured something else over it. "This is some of Aunt Harriet's magic formula," he told the assembled members. "We now have the secret that will keep Krinkle Krunch the number one cereal in America."

The news pleased the Board members. They applauded wildly. Then they chanted, "We're number one! We're number one! Krinkle's number one! We want Krinkle! We want Krinkle!"

Krinkle smiled broadly and tried to calm his overjoyed Board, but they continued to chant wildly. Finally, one Board member said stiffly, "Gentlemen! Gentlemen! I quite understand your enthusiastic response, but please let us have some semblance of order. Cereal history is about to be made."

"Thank you," Krinkle said, and the members settled back in their seats, preparing to witness history.

First Krinkle placed his spoon in the cereal bowl. Then he lifted the spoon to his mouth and took a bite. He chewed it, silently and thoughtfully. Then he took another bite. The Board members noticed something. It was subtle, but it was clear. This time he was chewing respectfully. A solemn look came over Krinkle's face. He stood, and the Board members stared, waiting to find out if it was history or cereal.

"Gentlemen," Krinkle said, relishing the gravity of his words, "it works."

The Board members stood and applauded, and Krinkle responded to the historical drama that was unfolding. "I can feel the blood rushing through my veins," he said. "It makes me feel so young, so strong, so vibrant."

His words filled the Board members with a new jubilation. Again they cheered wildly, as Krinkle flexed his muscles in response to their applause. Then he stepped up onto the table, as the Board members chanted: "Krinkle is the greatest! Krinkle is the greatest!"

Finally, one Board member broke through the chanting and said, "Krinkle, show us what you can do."

"Yes," another Board member added, "show us your strength, Krinkle."

Soon all the Board members picked up the idea and called for a show of strength. They calmed down when Krinkle raised his hands, asking them to be quiet.

"I know, men," Krinkle began. "It's one thing to have strength. It's another thing to prove it."

Again, Krinkle flexed his muscles and strutted around the table, trying to think of an appropriate gesture.

"The weights, Mr. Krinkle," one Board member called out.

"The weights," Krinkle said, glancing at some weights in the corner of the room. "I don't know why anyone brought weights. They're too easy."

Krinkle looked up at the chandelier, smiling as an idea came into his head. "Oh, not the lights, Mr. Krinkle," a board member called.

"Yes, I see what you mean," Krinkle answered, shrugging. "That would be undignified."

For a moment, Krinkle thought. Then he grinned and called out, "I have it!"

All attention focused on Krinkle at his place in front of the table. "Our inside man told me that Dean Higgins split that cheap crummy table of Harriet Crumply's with a karate chop. Can I do any less with this table?"

"No!" the Board members roared in approval.

"Stand back," Krinkle warned, "and look out for splinters."

Krinkle raised his hand in karate-chop style. Then he screamed "*yah,*" and brought his hand down, chopping hard at the table. It was a disaster — not for the table, but for Krinkle's hand! Krinkle screamed again, a horrible scream of pain, and the table didn't even bother to shake.

The meeting came to an abrupt end, skipping even the necessary motions, as several Board members had to help take Krinkle off to the hospital.

While Krinkle's hand was being X-rayed and bandaged, Harry was being driven to Arno and Cookie's rooming house. His men had come through, he thought, and they needed to share in the spoils.

Arno and Cookie were glad to see Harry. They were even happier when he showed them the money in hundred-dollar bills and counted it out into Arno's hand.

"Krinkle's putting on a show for his Board,"

"Yah," screams Krinkle as he attempts to split the table by using a karate chop. Krinkle screams again, a horrible scream of pain, and the table doesn't even bother to shake.

Harry told them. "I told him to call us when he's finished and share the good news with us."

"What kind of show is it?" Cookie asked.

Before Cookie could ask the next question that popped into his mind, the phone rang. "That must be him now," Harry said, cheerfully picking up the receiver.

Harry grinned. "Well, hello, Mr. Krinkle," he said. "I'm sure you had a wonderful day."

"It didn't work!" Krinkle screamed.

The grin came off Harry's face, and he grabbed the money out of Arno's hand. "What do you mean it didn't work?" he said into the receiver.

"I can prove it didn't work," Krinkle said. "And I'd like to get my hand on the two idiots you hired."

"Your hand?" Harry said.

"Forget that and think about this," Krinkle said. "If Medfield wins that weight-lifting contest, we're all going to be through. Can you imagine those skinny punks defeating a great team like State? It's ridiculous."

"Yeah, it's ridiculous," Harry agreed, pausing for a moment to think about the situation. "But look, Mr. Krinkle, if the formula doesn't work for us, then it doesn't work for them. It just means that Harriet Crumply is going to be destroyed, and she's going to have a bunch of weaklings eating her cereal with that formula in it on TV. Now, what if the sure winner, the greatest weight-lifting team in America, was seen eating Krinkle Krunch Cereal just before the match? What would that do for us on national TV?"

Harry visits Arno and Cookie. They are waiting for Mr. Krinkle's phone call. Harry is cheerful but Mr. Krinkle isn't grinning!

"Sounds all right to me," Krinkle agreed, "but you make sure that Medfield doesn't stumble onto the right formula again."

"I'll take care of it," Harry said. Then he hung up the receiver.

"How about our money?" Arno asked.

"I'll take care of it until after the match," Harry said.

"Why?" Arno asked. "What could happen?"

"Probably nothing," Harry concluded, "but you'd better have some boys lined up tonight just in case. Medfield had the right formula once, so let's make sure they don't get it again. Got me?"

"Got you," Arno said.

Then Harry left.

"I don't get it," Cookie said.

"I know," Arno answered, thinking about what he planned to do that night.

The Strongest Man In the World

CHAPTER NINE

The boys that Professor Quigley was able to recruit for the Medfield weight-lifting team were all shapes and sizes. They had one thing in common, though. Not one of them looked like a weight lifter.

A few hours before the evening of the nationally televised meet between Medfield and State, Medfield's weight lifters got stage fright. After seeing pictures of State's super strong team, common sense told them they were going to look like dumbbells trying to lift barbells.

Fortunately, Professor Quigley had secured a film of the feats of strength performed by Dean Higgins in Aunt Harriet's Board Room. He showed the film to the boys on his weight-lifting team, and it inspired them. They knew that if Schuyler's formula worked for Higgins, it would surely work for any normal person. "We'll murder State," they cheered and started for the gym.

People had already begun filing into the gym, and TV crews were setting up their cameras and checking other equipment. Most people didn't think Medfield had a chance, but they were curious. They figured the Medfield boys had something up their sleeves, because they surely didn't have anything in them.

When Dean Higgins arrived, he walked quickly to the section reserved for the Board of Regents. "Good evening, gentlemen," he said in greeting.

Turning to him, Regent Appleby said, "Higgins, I'm warning you. You've been dragging us to these sports contests for the last thirty years, and you've never had a winner. Well, this is your last chance."

Together, the other Regents added, "We're sick of it, Higgins."

"Well, I assure you, you won't be sick tonight," Higgins assured them.

Glancing over his glasses, Regent Appleby said, "Where's the team?"

Higgins looked around and spotted the team coming onto the gym floor. "Right there," he said proudly.

The sight of the Medfield team pulling off their sweatshirts caused Regent Appleby to cough violently. "That's the team?" he said, almost choking. "That bunch of wrecks?"

As the other Regents caught sight of the team, they, too, felt ill.

"I know they may not look like weight lifters," Higgins assured them, "but they'll surprise you."

"I'm surprised they're on their feet," one Regent said. "I've never seen anything like that."

Regent Appleby said, "They're the walking dead." Then he slumped back into his seat, overcome again by a siege of coughing.

Catching sight of Aunt Harriet, Higgins said,

"Just try to compose yourself, Regent Appleby. I'm sure you're going to enjoy yourself. Now excuse me. I have to go see Harriet Crumply."

Aunt Harriet and her Board of Directors were just getting seated when Higgins approached them. They were carrying pennants which read: "We're Number One," and Aunt Harriet was wearing an outfit that seemed as out of place in the gym as the Medfield team.

After shaking both of her hands, Higgins stepped back and said, "Aunt Harriet, you look like a dream tonight. Tell me, is this your victory gown?"

Obviously pleased, Aunt Harriet smiled and said, "It's just a little something I picked up."

Then Aunt Harriet glanced onto the gym floor at the Medfield weight lifters. They looked miserable, and a delighted smile came over Aunt Harriet's face. "Just the way I pictured them, gentlemen," she said to the Board. "Someone we all know is going to be very surprised today."

That "someone" was Krinkle, and to Aunt Harriet's surprise, he appeared behind her and slapped her on the back. "Well, Harriet Crumply," he said, "you old son of a gun."

Krinkle's Board members were with him, and they, too, were carrying "We're Number One" pennants. "I see my team's working out," Krinkle said. "And where's your team, Harriet?"

Harriet reluctantly pointed to the Medfield weight lifters, who were going through what might loosely be called exercises.

"Oh," Krinkle said, trying to hide the shock. "Well, good luck, Harriet."

Harriet thanked him, and after he had gone,

Higgins said to her, "Don't pay any attention to him, Harriet. This is our night."

The gym was filling up, and the excitement of the night's event was filling the air. The signal had just been passed to the ace TV sports announcer Gene Durante that the national broadcast could be started, and looking into the camera, he said, "Well, ladies and gentlemen of TV Land, it looks like we are about to begin this much publicized match of the century."

Pausing, Durante was handed a note by one of the TV crew. He read it through. Then he said, "Oh, incidentally, I've just received a note from out network director requesting that you not try to adjust your sets in any way. You are having no video problem. I repeat, you are having no video problem. That really is the Medfield team you see out there warming up."

The scene shifted to the stage where Aunt Harriet and Krinkle were standing and bowing to the crowd. Then both of them turned to their respective teams, who seated themselves at the tables where they had been standing and began eating the bowls of cereal in front of them.

Durante couldn't believe his eyes. "Well, ladies and gentlemen," he told his TV audience, "I heard rumors that we might have a few surprises this evening. Well, I'm surprised already. I'm not sure whether we're having a weight-lifting match, or a cereal eating contest. Well, if the Medfield boys can lift weights as well as they can toss cereal down their throats, State is going to find itself in a tough contest."

The Medfield team was eating quickly and joyfully. The boys felt as if Schuyler's formula

To the victor the spoils! Aunt Harriet and Krinkle bow to the crowd. Each one is certain of victory. But both teams can't win.

was giving them the strength they needed. But one boy was eating slowly and thoughtfully. It was Dexter. He had been the first person to try Schuyler's formula, and he could see that there was no smoke pouring out of his nostrils...or any other nostrils, for that matter.

Then the boys raced for the gym floor, and one boy called to Dexter, "Come on! We're ready to kill State."

"I'll be right with you," Dexter said, taking his cereal bowl with him and following slowly after his excited teammates.

From across the floor, the State weight lifters watched in bewilderment. The Medfield boys had jumped into some weird exercises. Their enthusiasm made the muscular State lifters wonder if they could possibly have some kind of secret weapon.

Dexter also had some doubts. He walked over to Quigley, who was standing off to the side watching the team, along with Harry and Schuyler.

Noticing the look of concern on Dexter's face and the bowl in his hands, Schuyler said, "What's the matter, Dexter?"

"We're in trouble," Dexter said. "The formula doesn't work."

"How can you say it doesn't work?" Quigley asked, pointing to the team. "Look at them."

"You look at them," Dexter said. "They're just carried away. They're all psyched up, but I tell you, I know. Those guys aren't any stronger. There's something missing in the formula. There's no blue smoke."

"Wait a second," Harry said. "I don't care

about blue smoke or anything else. Our company has a fortune tied up in that stuff, and this thing is on national TV. Now don't tell me your team's not going to win!"

"Just a minute, Harry," Quigley said. "The school and these kids have something at stake, too. Now what do you think is wrong, Dexter?"

Dexter took another bite of the cereal and thought for a moment. Then he smiled. "I have it," he said, swallowing the cereal. "It had an acid taste before."

"That's impossible," Schuyler corrected. "A vitamin formula like mine wouldn't have an acid taste."

Dexter thought hard, allowing past events to spin through his mind. Fixing on some key moments, he said, "Remember the day all the stuff got knocked over in the lab? And remember the day the cow gave all the milk? It was the day before I ate the cereal and got strong. Well, somehow my formula got mixed up with the cereal. My formula had an acid taste, and it was my formula that gave the strength, not the vitamins."

"You mean my formula didn't have anything to do with it?" Schuyler asked sadly.

Before Dexter could answer, a bell rang and the floor was cleared. The contest was beginning. A State lifter stepped into the spotlight and flexed his muscles. He was a giant. "The first contestant for State," the announcer said, "will be Artemus Jusko attempting two hundred pounds."

Time was running out. "I don't know what happened," Dexter told Schuyler. "But I do know that we don't have the right formula now, and if we want to win, I'd better get to the lab and get the right one in a hurry."

All this time, Harry had been listening carefully. "Good idea," he told Dexter. "I'm glad you're going to do something about it. You'll have to excuse me. I have something to do, but you get going, young man. You get out to the lab."

Harry walked off, leaving Dexter, Quigley, and Schuyler wondering where Dexter would get a car for his trip to the lab. The three of them had no reason to suspect Harry. They had no reason to believe that he was going off to call Arno. But he was.

The Strongest Man In the World

CHAPTER TEN

Without thinking, Dean Higgins gave his car keys to Dexter. The Dean was sitting with Regent Dietz and trying to assure the Regent that the two hundred pounds which Jusko lifted for State was nothing, compared to what Medfield was going to do.

"And now, the first contestant for Medfield," the floor announcer called. "He is Charles 'Porky' Peterson, and will be attempting two hundred and seventy-five pounds."

Porky strutted out onto the floor and bowed to the cheering Medfield fans. Porky spent most of his time lifting forks and spoons, but the cereal had given him new confidence. He felt like a bull. He strutted some more, to the delight of the Medfield fans.

Unfortunately, the sight of Porky didn't delight Regent Appleby. He turned to Higgins and said, "What is that thing? He's not lifting weights for us, is he?"

"Well, ah, Porky," Higgins said, trying to bring himself to applaud. "I mean Charles. He doesn't look too good, but you just watch. You just watch."

Durante, the TV announcer, was watching.

"As you in TV Land will notice," he said, "the Medfield contestant is a little out of shape. But don't let that fool you. Remember — the cardinal rule of any sport is not the muscle you have, but how you use it."

Finally, Porky got set and stood over the barbell. He took a deep breath and then snorted like a pig. He bent for the weight and lifted. The barbell didn't move. A slight look of surprise came over Porky's face, but he tried again. Perspiration ran down Porky's face. He realized that he couldn't lift the weight!

"From here it looks like Peterson is having a little bit more of a problem than he thought," Durante told his TV audience.

Porky made one big last effort, and, in a way, it was rewarded. He didn't budge the weight, but his arms came out of their sockets, proving that he had tried.

Porky stood up straight. His arms hung down to the floor. He looked like an ape — an overweight ape. He turned and walked off with his arms dangling by his ankles.

The remaining Medfield lifters were shocked. They were drained of their confidence. And in the seating area, the Regents were beating Higgins with their canes until he had to flee from his seat. He ran into the section where Harriet was sitting, and he saw she was crying.

In the meantime, Durante had just received a message from a member of the TV crew, and he was saying, "We have a report on the last Medfield contestant, Peterson. He's all right. Evidently, he just suffered a stretched muscle or two, but he's pulling himself together."

Porky tries to budge the bar, but the bar budges him. Now his arms reach all the way down to his ankles. Can this be the start of something good?

Durante wasn't kidding, because as he continued to talk the TV cameras settled on Porky, and, sure enough, his arms were sliding slowly back into their sockets. "Our next contestant will be Glen Harlan from State." Durante told the viewers.

The State fans cheered as Harlan walked over to a loaded barbell. Harlan's build was magnificent, and watching him, sadly, was the Medfield team. Harlan quickly jerked the bar to his chest and then easily pressed two hundred and seventy-five pounds overhead.

"Now that's what I call weight lifting," Emmet "Shorty" Perkins, a member of the Medfield team, said in awe.

His words caught the ear of Higgins who had come down to the bench to find out what was going on. He turned on Shorty and said, "Of course that's weight lifting, and if we had a coach, we'd have a weight lifter instead of a freak with elastic arms."

"That's unfair," Quigley said. "I told our boys that once they ate the formula, they would become supermen."

"I know," Higgins agreed, "but where are the supermen? Those clowns haven't changed a bit."

"The formula doesn't work," Quigley admitted. "Dexter thinks there's been a mix-up, and he's back at the lab trying to get it straightened out."

"Well, he'd better hurry," Higgins said, "but not too much. He has my car!"

The next Medfield lifter also failed to get the

barbell off the floor. He was followed by State's Ben Farrell, a giant who pressed three hundred and fifty pounds. The score was State 825, Medfield 0.

Higgins groaned. "Quigley," he said, "what are we going to do? The Board of Regents looks like they'd like to eat me alive."

"Well, we have Slither coming up next," Quigley said hopefully. "He's pretty good."

"Who told you that?" Higgins asked.

"He did," Quigley whispered.

In a way, Slither *was* pretty good. After much struggling, he managed to get one hundred pounds over head. Then his arms locked. He couldn't let go of the bar, and he began to stagger all over the gym.

"His muscles seem to have frozen!" Durante yelled to the TV audience, as the cameras tried to follow the staggering Slither. "He can't let go of the barbell. Uh-oh, there he goes!"

Slither finally staggered to a stop at the center of the platform, but the weight was too much for him. He fell backward, still holding the barbell.

Other Medfield lifters raced onto the platform. They pried Slither from the barbell and stood him up. His arms were frozen straight up in the air, and his teammates frantically tried to lower them. It was no use — they wouldn't budge. Slither walked off the platform with his arms raised over his head.

The score flashed. It was State 825, Medfield 100.

Things were looking bad for Medfield, for

Dean Higgins, and for Aunt Harriet. All hope rested on Dexter, and things weren't looking too good for him either.

Dexter had reached the lab, all right. He had found a test tube filled with the formula. He tested it slightly and couldn't be sure that it would work, but he stuffed the corked tube inside his sweater. He'd see if it worked when he got back to the gym. "Maybe it only works with the cereal," he told himself, and turned toward the lab door.

All of a sudden, all the lab lights came on. Arno, Cookie, and a bunch of other hoods were standing by the door. "Okay, Dexter," Arno said menacingly, "we'll take that formula."

"It doesn't work," Dexter said pleadingly.

"That's all right," Arno said. "We'll take it anyway. Get him, boys!"

Dexter raced for the door, and one of the hoods tackled him. The others piled on. In seconds, Dexter disappeared under a sea of sprawling bodies, and with him, all hope for Medfield seemed to disappear, too.

The Strongest Man In the World

CHAPTER ELEVEN

Beneath the pile of hoods, Dexter reached into his sweater and pulled out the test tube with the formula in it. The formula hadn't worked a moment ago, but in desperation, Dexter took another sip of the liquid. It was his only chance.

Seconds later, blue smoke was pouring out of Dexter's nostrils and new strength was pulsing through his veins. It worked!

By ones and twos, Dexter tossed the crooks off. They came fighting back, but they were no match for Dexter. He knocked all of them, including Arno and Cookie, into semi-consciousness. Then he turned and ran from the room.

As Dexter raced down the corridor for the stairs, something in the shadows caught his eye. He turned and saw Harry with fear written all over his face.

"Oh, so it's you," Dexter said, moving toward Harry.

"Now leave me alone," Harry bubbled. "You have no right to touch me."

Dexter grabbed Harry by the collar and said, "It was you all the time! You were behind it all the time, weren't you?"

By ones and twos, Dexter tosses the crooks off. They're no match for Dexter and his amazing formula.

"I'm warning you," Harry said weakly. "Let me go."

Dexter looked down the hall and saw Arno, Cookie, and the other hoods running toward him in a formation that resembled the setup for bowling pins.

"Hey, fellows," Dexter called down the corridor. "Here's your captain!"

Before the hoods could spread out, Dexter slid Harry across the floor at them, and Harry crashed into the pack, knocking all of the men off their feet.

"Strike!" Dexter called, snapping his fingers and then racing off down the stairs.

At the same time, there was another crash at the gym. It was the crash of a three hundred and fifty pound barbell that had just been successfully lifted by Jon Shepard of State.

"Well, that was quite a lift by mighty Jon Shepard," Durante, the TV announcer, said. "I'm sorry that the people listening to this by radio couldn't see it. Shepard is amazing. The score now is State 1175, Medfield 100. Medfield's last contestant and last hope is Dexter Riley. In order for Medfield to win, Dexter will have to lift over one thousand pounds. Now you'll have to excuse me, folks, but I'm going to hold my hand over the mike and make believe you can't hear me laughing."

But his laughter came through, and as he was laughing, a member of the TV crew handed Durante a note. He read it and laughed again.

"Excuse me, folks," Durante chuckled to his audience. "I just received a report that Dexter's out for an equipment repair. Well, it's going to be hard for him to get a new body now. Most of the stores are closed tonight."

Again, Durante laughed, and this time Dexter, who was trying to start the car and had turned the radio on, heard him. Angry, Dexter made another try at starting the car. Then he listened to the radio again as Durante said, "Well, we finally have a ruling. The referee is allowing Medfield's Dexter Riley exactly four minutes to appear and lift the one thousand and seventy-five pounds. Dean Higgins insisted on the grace period, and I would guess that if Riley arrives here with a derrick, he has a chance."

"Four minutes," Dexter said, banging his hand on the steering wheel. "How can I get there in four minutes?"

Dexter closed his eyes, hoping that an answer would come to him, and, sure enough, it did. His eyes popped open and glittered with joy. He leaped out of the car, pulling the test tube from his pocket as he moved. At the rear of the car, he poured some of the formula into the gas tank, and just as he settled back into the driver's seat, he heard Harry call out, "There he goes! Get him!"

Dexter started the car and it responded with new power. A cloud of black smoke poured out of its exhaust into the faces of the oncoming crooks, and the car ripped away from the curb.

Terror gripped Dexter. The car was moving through traffic like the mightiest racer of the road, but its parts were flying off, and to top everything, a police car was following him.

A red light signal came up before Dexter. He hit the brake and his right foot went through the floor. Then he pulled the emergency brake, and it tore off in his hand. Desperately, Dexter slammed his left foot through the floorboard and pulled hard on the steering wheel. It bent in his hands, but he managed to get his feet on the pavement and bring the car to a skidding stop.

The police car pulled up behind Dexter, and the two policemen got out and approached him. Unfortunately, he had trouble on his hands: the car wanted to go. Its back wheels were spinning, and Dexter was holding on to the steering wheel with all the strength he could muster.

"May I see your operator's license?" one policeman asked.

"I'm afraid I left it in my clothes back at the gym," Dexter said.

"That only makes it worse, kid," the policeman said, taking out his ticket book and moving toward the back of the car. "I hope you have license plates on this thing."

At the rear of the car, the policeman noticed that the license was covered with soot. "Say, Charley," he called to his partner, "will you wipe this plate off for me? I can't read it."

While the policemen worked on the license plate, Dexter's attention turned to the radio. Durante said, "Well, folks, we're down to our final two minutes. If Dexter Riley doesn't appear and perform by that time, it will be all over for Medfield. And if Dexter Riley *does* appear and perform by that time, it will still probably be all over for Medfield."

Dexter looked up and saw that the light had changed to green. "Excuse me," he called apologetically to the policemen, "but I have to go."

Then Dexter released his grip on the wheel and lifted his feet off the ground. The car zoomed off, belching black smoke and soot all over the policemen. As it flew down the street, its hood and other parts came soaring back at the bewildered officers.

At the gym, Aunt Harriet was at the end of her patience. "Now you hear this and hear this well, Higgins," she said. "You've ruined me—you and that phony formula of yours! Well, you're not going to get away with it. You might just as well plan on closing up that hokey little school of yours, because you're going to jail, Higgins. You're going to jail for a long time."

"Jail!" Higgins said in dismay. "You wouldn't send me to jail, Aunt Harriet."

"Don't you Aunt Harriet me!" she screamed. "I'd send you to jail in a minute!"

Krinkle appeared on the scene then, and smiling victoriously, he said, "Problems, Harriet?"

"Problems?" Harriet said, changing her tone completely. "We don't have any problems, do we, Dean Higgins?"

Higgins forced out a laugh and said, "Why, no, of course not."

"How could you have any problems?" Krinkle said, joining them in laughter. "The meet's over."

"The meet is not over," Higgins said.

"Where's Riley?" the referee yelled to Higgins.

"Don't yell at me!" Higgins shot back. "I told you he was out for equipment repairs."

"Well, he'd better get back here in a hurry,"

Smugly, Krinkle enjoys the embarrassing defeat of Medfield College and his rival, Crumply Crunch Cereal.

the referee warned. "He has only fifty-eight seconds left."

Turning to Krinkle, Higgins said, "I told you the meet wasn't over. We have fifty-eight seconds left."

"Why don't you call off this farce?" the referee asked. "That kid's not out for equipment repairs, and you know it. He's run out on you."

"How dare you, sir," Krinkle said, playfully acting shocked. "If Dean Wiggins says the boy is out for equipment repairs, the boy is out for equipment repairs."

"Higgins, not Wiggins," the Dean said.

"This is ridiculous," the referee told Krinkle. "The kid's not coming. Your team has won."

"My team has not won," Krinkle said, enjoying the tick-tock of defeat playing upon Harriet's ears. "Krinkle is always fair. We still have forty-five seconds left, and anything can happen in forty-five seconds. Right, Harriet?"

Krinkle's burst of laughter was muffled quickly by the sound of a car crashing into the building. He turned and saw a car come skidding to a stop in the center of the floor.

"My car!" Higgins cried in horror.

"Don't worry about it," Dexter said, jumping out of the car. "It's just a matter of replacing a few parts."

The Medfield team, led by Quigley, raced over to Dexter. "Did you get the right formula?" Quigley asked.

"Sure I got the right formula," Dexter said.

The team cheered, as Dexter quickly pulled his sweatshirt over his head. There was still time, but not much!

The Strongest Man in the World

CHAPTER TWELVE

The barbell weighed one thousand and seventy-six pounds. If Dexter pressed it, Medfield would win the meet, but no man had ever lifted that much weight overhead.

Dexter trotted over to the barbell and glanced quickly at the clock. It was ticking away. After a deep breath, he bent over and reached for the weight. It wouldn't budge. He tried hard, but it wouldn't budge. He was in trouble.

"Watch that clock, ref," Krinkle yelled.

"I have to get some cereal," Dexter called, as he ran from the floor to the cereal area.

The referee ran after Dexter and nearly collided with Higgins. "He's eating more cereal," the referee complained. "What are you trying to do to us?"

"I'm not trying to do anything to anyone," Higgins answered.

Moving to the curtain which shielded the cereal area from his view, the ref called, "Come on, kid, you have less than twenty seconds."

Suddenly a puff of blue smoke came from behind the curtain. It was followed by Dexter who raced by Higgins and the ref.

Still surprised by the smoke, the referee said, "What was that?"

"Oh that was Dexter Riley," Higgins explained. "He's a member of our weight-lifting team."

Dexter almost raced by the barbell, too, except that he tripped over it. He fell to the floor, stunned. Higgins and Schuyler tried to get him to his feet, while Aunt Harriet tried to keep from fainting. Dexter shook off his helpers and managed to get to his feet. At the barbell, he took another deep breath and glanced at the clock. It read five seconds. This was it!

Dexter pulled the weight to his chest. The bar was bending in the middle from the tremendous amount of weight at each end, and it didn't seem to be moving as easy as Dexter thought it would move. Again, he looked at the clock. It read: Three seconds.

Dexter pressed with every ounce of strength he had. Up moved the weight. When it was overhead, Dexter locked his arms in place and waited for the referee's signal. "Good lift," the referee signaled.

"He did it!" Durante screamed out to his TV audience. "He did it! Medfield has won the meet! And Dexter Riley is the strongest man in the world!"

The Medfield students went wild with joy. First they lifted Dexter to their shoulders. Next, at Dexter's insistence, Schuyler was hoisted up into the air. Finally, they lifted Higgins into the air.

While Medfield was celebrating, Krinkle was eating. He had slipped behind the curtain in the cereal area and was gulping down what remained of the Crumply cereal.

Dexter pulls the weight above his chest. The bar bends in the middle. Will he get it all the way up?

Seated on the shoulders of some of her Board members, Aunt Harriet wrote out a check and passed it to Higgins. Higgins' eyes almost popped when he read it. He blew Harriet a kiss —his job was saved. Even the Regents were happy!

And in defeat Krinkle, too, thought he was happy. He had eaten all of Harriet's cereal that he could find. He hadn't gotten any smoke out of it, but he was ready. He could feel it. He raised his hand over the table and gave it a tremendous karate chop. As the pain raced up his arm, he let out a terrific scream. With no smoke, it's no joke!